Beast Quest ®

Falra
THE SNOW PHOENIX

BY ADAM BLADE

ORCHARD

THE CENTRAL PLAINS

THE NORTHERN MOUNTAINS

THE FOREST OF FEAR

GRASSY PLAINS

WESTERN OCEAN

THE CITY OF SNAKES

THE WINDIN

THE RUBY DESERT

SPINDREL

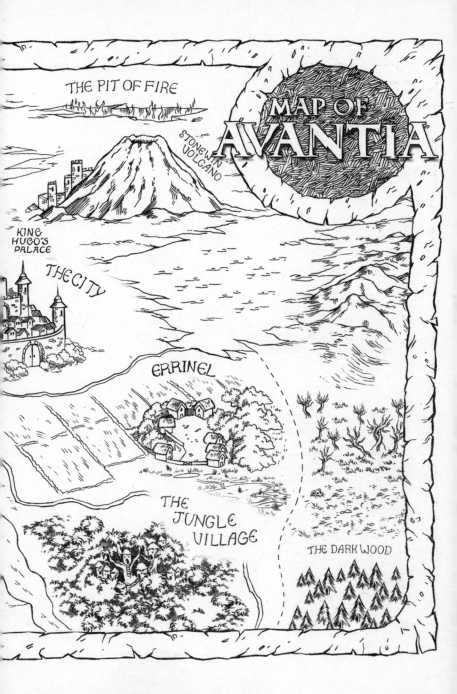

CONTENTS

Dear reader,

Do not pity me – my spells may be useless now, but my sixth sense will never go. Evil is afoot in this once peaceful kingdom. Jezrin the Judge may have been defeated by brave Tom, but his minions do not rest. Our many Quests have taught me that an enemy beaten back will return stronger than before.

Tonight I had a vision of the pale moon turning black. What it means is not clear, but a new menace stalks the land of Rion, and I fear it will spread to Avantia. My wizard instincts tell me that our enemies plan to tip the balance of nature, turning Good to Evil. A hero will be needed to stand against the dark forces. Can you guess who that hero might be?

Aduro, former wizard to King Hugo

PROLOGUE

"I remember the first time I walked the Stonewin Trail," said Nikolus. "It must have been fifty years ago."

"Oh, yes?" said Shay. *Here comes one of Grandpa's stories,* he thought. "On a Quest, I suppose. Finding some treasure, rescuing a maiden, fighting monsters for the king?"

Shay's grandfather paused, leaning heavily on Shay's arm. "Actually, it was on a march to fight the armies of Rion," he said. "My armour glinted in the sunlight, my sword was sharp enough to cut through a tree trunk…"

Shay smiled and let his mind drift, staring out over the fields bordering the road. Far off, he saw the heat haze blurring the sky above the Pit of Fire.

Grandpa's rambling, he thought. Despite his wild claims, Nikolus had never been a knight at all. He'd raised cattle all his life on the same farm, just like his father before him.

Shay winced as his blistered feet throbbed. They'd been walking the Stonewin Trail, from Avantia's famous volcano to the borders of

Rion, for three days. Each day his grandfather struggled on, relying more and more on Shay to keep him on his feet.

We can't stop, though, Shay thought. Nikolus needed to get to the steaming pools by the Pit of Fire. They made the trip once a year. Those green waters, naturally heated by the volcano, were the only thing that soothed his aching bones.

"...deadly battle," his grandfather was saying. "The knights of Rion were tough, but finally they surrendered."

Shay saw the faraway look in his grandfather's eyes.

Does he really believe what he's saying? he wondered.

"Not far now," Shay said. "Look,

there are the Caves of Echoes!"

While the fields south of the road stretched as far as the eye could see, the fields to the north gave way to rocks, with dark holes leading into caverns and tunnels. Travellers on the Stonewin Trail often used the caves to shelter from bad weather, but they gave Shay the chills. Who knew what lived in their dark corners?

As they passed the first of the cave mouths, Shay noticed something odd in the fields opposite. The wild grasses seemed to be covered with ash.

"Ever seen anything like that before?" Shay asked, pointing.

His grandfather frowned. "Must have been that great white bird," he said.

Shay groaned. "Not again, Grandpa!"

Since yesterday morning, Nikolus had claimed more than once that he'd seen a giant bird in the sky ahead, circling the Pit of Fire. But whenever Shay had looked up, there was nothing there.

"Don't believe me, then," grumbled his grandfather. "Nothing to be afraid of," he added, drawing out a necklace of dingy, grey beads. "I've got just the thing to fight it."

He waved the beads before his face.

"I'm glad you've got those," said Shay, grinning. "If I was an imaginary bird, I'd be really scared."

Nikolus's face was suddenly serious. "Imaginary!" he said. "What do you call that, then?"

He pointed. Shay followed the line of his finger and gasped. *It can't be...*

Soaring over the Pit of Fire was a gleaming white bird. Its wingspan must have been fifty paces, its talons large enough to snatch a bullock from a field. The creature folded its wings and dived into the Pit.

Surely it will be killed, thought Shay.

A moment later the bird rose into the air again, its wings dripping with lava, feathers streaked black and red. It shrieked in triumph.

"A phoenix!" said his grandfather. "Fire can't harm it."

The Beast tipped its wings, scattering ash from its beak and talons. Then it flew right towards Shay and his grandfather. The falling ash sparked fires in the fields below.

"Stand back, my boy," shouted Nikolus, holding his beads aloft. "This is a job for a knight."

"Run!" said Shay.

He wrapped an arm around his grandfather's shoulders and pulled

him towards the nearest of the caves. Shay bundled Nikolus quickly into the cave mouth, just as the shadow of the flying Beast fell over him. A huge cloud of ash and smoke, like a solid wall, blasted towards them.

"We have to go deeper!" said Shay. His grandfather stumbled, falling to the ground with a cry. Shay could feel the heat of the deadly ash on his skin. Darkness fell as the smoke blocked out the sun. "Come on!" he said. He helped his grandfather up none too gently and pulled the old man along by the arm.

Coughing and blind, Shay went deeper into the Caves of Echoes.

He wondered if he'd ever see the daylight again.

1

THE FINAL BEAST

Tom slashed his blade through the
snaking vines. Sweat poured off his
face and his tunic stuck to his back.
Imma, a girl of the tree people, had
shown them the way to go. It was her
way of saying thank you, after they
had liberated Tikron, a giant monkey
that had been terrorising the jungle.

*But we're wasting time even
so,* Tom thought. *There's one*

more Quest to face and we're still struggling out of the jungle.

Finally, he saw clear daylight ahead.

"This way!" he called to the others. "We're almost there."

Elenna led Silver and Storm through the dense foliage. Soon they reached the edge of the trees. Tom unfolded the map given to him by the wizard, Aduro. He pointed to the far north of the kingdom.

"This is where we need to go next," he said.

"The Pit of Fire," Elenna read from the label on the map.

"It's the perfect lair for Falra the Snow Phoenix," said Tom.

Falra, who was once our friend. But now she's our enemy.

Tom folded the map and stuffed it away angrily. Kensa had stooped to new depths, turning Good Beasts to Evil. She'd cast a spell over young Beasts from Rion, those unable to protect themselves. So far he'd managed to free three of them – Tikron, Vislak and Raffkor. Only Falra remained in Kensa's thrall.

It wasn't just Falra's life at stake. Kensa had poisoned the twin dragons, Vedra and Krimon, with lunar blood. Krimon had succumbed, and his brother was stricken. With every day that passed, the Evil spread through his veins. By that very night, the transformation would be complete. The only way to cure him was by mixing four ingredients, each guarded by a Beast of Rion. Tom had claimed three, but Falra guarded the fourth.

And if I know Kensa, the final fight will be the most deadly.

Storm shook a vine free of his hooves and reared up.

"Someone's glad to be out of the jungle," said Elenna. She stooped to stroke Silver's back, but the wolf bared his teeth and growled. "What's got into you?" she asked.

Tom felt his skin prickle and the hairs on his neck rose. He quickly drew his sword half out of his scabbard, as the air seemed to wobble. A shape was appearing...

"Daltec!" he cried with relief, sheathing his sword.

The wizard's face was serious.

"You must hurry!" he said, striding towards them. "Vedra's condition becomes more and more severe. His scales...they're almost completely black now."

"We'll ride to the Pit of Fire at once," Tom said grimly.

"It's too far," said Daltec. "Even for Storm at full gallop. You'll never make it there, then back to the palace before nightfall."

"Can't you magic us closer to the Pit of Fire?" asked Elenna.

"Perhaps," said Daltec, "but it's a long way, and there are four of you…"

"Please try!" said Tom.

"It's dangerous," said Daltec, twisting his robes with a nervous hand. "You might come to harm if my magic isn't strong enough."

Tom glanced at Elenna. She gave him a firm nod, as though reading his thoughts. "Forget the risks," he said determinedly. "We can't let Kensa's plan succeed!"

Daltec nodded. "I need you all to

face north, in the direction of travel."

Tom tugged Storm's head around, and planted his feet north. Elenna stood at his side with Silver.

"Good luck," said Daltec. He raised his hands towards them, took a deep breath and closed his eyes. His lips moved in a silent spell.

Golden light sparked across the wizard's fingertips, then shot towards Tom and his companions. A white orb surrounded them. Through it, Tom saw the landscape drain of colour. A frown crossed the young wizard's face, growing into a grimace of pain. The light from his hands came in waves, flashing and dying.

"He can't do it," whispered Elenna. "He's not strong enough!"

Daltec gritted his teeth, his whole body starting to shake. Golden sparks scattered around them.

A roar erupted from the wizard and blinding light made Tom clamp shut his eyes.

Then all went silent.

When Tom dared to open his eyes again, he saw that the Dark Jungle and Daltec had vanished. Now Tom and Elenna were standing in the middle of a wide path that was scored with cart trails.

"Where are we?" asked Elenna.

Tom glanced back. In the far distance, barely a shadow, rose the Stonewin volcano. Ahead of them, the air seemed to shift, as if the sun were beating down hard. But dark clouds filled the sky completely, blocking out any of the sun's rays. *The heat must be coming from below – the Pit of Fire!*

"We're on the Stonewin Trail," he said. "Daltec did it!"

He patted Storm's neck, hope surging through his veins.

"Oh, no!" Elenna cried.

Tom turned to his friend, and saw that she had raised her hands to her face in dismay.

A heartbeat later, he understood why.

Silver was nowhere to be seen.

DEADLY SKIES

"Silver!" Elenna cried, turning on the spot. "Silver, where are you?"

Tom remembered Daltec's words about the risk involved. He put his hand on Elenna's shoulder. "He didn't make it," he said quietly. "Perhaps he turned around at the last moment. If he was facing a different way, Daltec's magic would have taken him somewhere else in the kingdom."

"I suppose so," said Elenna, a brief spark of hope burning in her eyes.

"Try not to worry," said Tom. "Silver can look after himself."

"You're right. And there's a Quest to complete," said Elenna, shaking herself. "Let's go."

Tom climbed onto Storm, and helped his friend up behind him. He gave the stallion's flanks a nudge and they galloped along the trail towards the Pit of Fire.

It wasn't long before they saw the outskirts of a village in the distance. Tom checked the map and saw the place's name.

"Tamas," he said. "Perhaps we'll find someone who's seen the Beast."

But as they rode into the town,

Tom's blood ran cold. *We'll find no people here*, he thought.

Tamas was deserted, the buildings half destroyed. It looked like a fire had caught hold, taking many of the houses and shops with it. Beams and timbers were blackened or reduced to charcoal. Smoke still hung in the air,

and Storm's hooves kicked up ash.

"This must be Falra's doing," said Elenna. "The poor people!"

As they pressed on through a charred orchard, the smoke thickened and became hotter, and a gusting wind threw ashy flakes across their path. Tom began to cough.

"I'm not sure we can keep going through this," he said.

"Wait a moment," said Elenna. "I've got an idea."

Tom drew Storm to a halt, and his friend slipped out of the saddle. Without speaking, she gripped his sword hilt and heaved the blade from his scabbard.

"What—?" Tom began.

"I need to borrow it," said Elenna.

"Trust me."

She went to the nearest tree. Its trunk was black and flaking. Elenna used the sword point to slice away a large section of bark. The flames had made it stiff.

"Good thinking!" said Tom, understanding. "Another shield!"

Elenna took the bark to a small stream running through the centre of the orchard and dipped it in the water. "If it's soaked through, it'll withstand more heat," she said, carrying the bark to Tom and Storm.

She gave Tom his sword, and he climbed down from Storm.

"It won't protect us from fire," Elenna said, "but it should keep these horrid black flakes at bay."

Tom stuck his sword into one end of the bark shield, and Elenna jammed an arrow in the other. Together, they hoisted it ahead of them. Guiding Storm slowly, they pushed on out of the abandoned village. Tom could barely see ten paces ahead for most of the way. Occasionally the smoke cleared long enough to see the Pit of Fire in the distance, but then it would close in again like a black cloak wrapping around them.

The shield worked. *But we won't be able to hold it up forever,* thought Tom.

They passed ash-scalded meadows of dead grass and flowers. Tom sighed at the devastation. *The crops will take years to recover.*

Soon the road dipped into a rocky gorge, pockmarked with caves. The route picked its way along a snaking path through a boulder field. Tom checked the map. "We need to keep heading north," he said. "We should leave the path – it'll be quicker."

So they set off over rough ground.

The ash clouds thinned out, because there was no vegetation or wood to burn in the barren landscape. Tom lowered the shield, grateful to give his aching arms a rest.

A sudden cry rang out.

"What was that?" asked Elenna.

Tom strained his ears. Had they found Falra already?

He heard the cry again. A wail of panic, or pain, off to their left. "Help me!" someone cried.

"It sounds like a boy," Tom said. "We must go to him. Come on!"

He followed the sound, scrambling over rocky ground. He knew that with every step he was heading further from his Quest – but he couldn't leave a child to suffer.

Maybe it's just someone who's got lost, he thought. *We can help them and be on our way again in no time.*

"Please, help!" called the voice again.

Tom and Elenna reached a dark cave mouth. Tom was about to go in when he felt a blast of heat. "Something's burning fiercely in there," he said. "Elenna, pass me the bark shield."

"You can't go in there!" she said. "It's far too dangerous."

As she spoke, Tom heard scuffing footsteps. A moment later, a small, raggedy boy came running out of the cave mouth. His face and clothes were smeared with soot. He saw them and fell to his knees, coughing. "Please!" he begged. "Help me!"

Tom ran to his side, and helped the boy to his feet. "Don't worry," he said. "You're safe now."

Peering into the cave, he saw a dim orange light flicker deep within. Bitter smoke reached his nostrils. *Fire!*

"You don't understand," said the boy, pulling free of Tom's grip. Tears smudged his blackened cheeks. "My grandfather's in there! He's collapsed in the smoke. I'm not strong enough! I couldn't drag him out. Will you help us?"

With the heat baking his face, Tom glanced at Elenna. He knew from her worried eyes that she was thinking the same thing as him.

If we go in there, we'll die.

1

3

TRIAL BY FIRE

Tom took a step closer to the cave entrance. Dark smoke had begun to drift out of it.

Elenna caught his arm. "You mustn't do this!" she said.

Tom looked from the boy's anguished face to his friend.

"But we can't let an old man die," he said.

"If you go in, you might both die,"

said Elenna. "And then who will battle Falra?"

Tom unbuckled his sword belt and handed it to Elenna. Her brow creased in confusion.

"If I don't make it out," he said, "take Storm and finish the Quest."

The stallion snorted and tossed his head. *This isn't goodbye,* Tom thought, and patted his horse's neck.

He ran towards the cave entrance, raising his shield and summoning the power of Ferno's dragon scale. At once, the deadly heat dropped, pushed back by the scale's enchantment. But it did nothing about the choking smoke. Tom dropped into a crawl, staying near the floor where there was more air. Gritty ash filled his eyes, almost blinding him. *How far in is the boy's grandfather?* Already he could barely see six paces ahead. Flames licked the walls not far off. *Could anyone really survive down here? Perhaps Elenna was right...*

His hands found something. Rough material, then an arm. Tom forced his watering eyes to open and saw a man lying on the ground, on his front. He was still breathing, but only just.

Bending down, Tom hooked his arms under the man's armpits and heaved him upright.

"You have to stand!" he shouted into the man's ear.

But the old man was unconscious. So Tom bent his knees and hoisted the man over his shoulder, legs

trembling under the weight. A fit of
coughing shook him, but he managed
to stay on his feet. Holding his shield
aloft to fend off the worst of the
heat, he shambled backwards out of
the cave. He hoped he was heading
the right way – the smoke billowing

all around made it hard to be sure. He tripped and fell into a wall, but righted himself. Then he saw dim light. Each breath scorched his lungs. *I won't last much longer*, he thought.

Tom stumbled towards the daylight. Through the smoke, he made out the boy and Elenna rushing in his direction. With the last of his strength, Tom laid the man on the ground, then collapsed, spluttering.

The boy fell beside his grandfather, taking him by the shoulders. "Grandpa, are you all right? It's me, Shay. Can you open your eyes?"

Elenna helped Tom to stand.

"What's your grandfather's name?" she asked the boy.

Storm was circling them, shaking

his mane and whinnying anxiously.

"Nikolus," the boy said, stroking the old man's arm. "I told him we should never have made this journey. The Pit of Fire is so far, and…"

The white-haired old man stirred, half sitting. He started to cough violently, each spasm making his whole body shake. When the fit had passed he looked around himself in confusion. "Shay?" he said. "Who are these people?"

The boy smiled. "They saved you from the fire," he said.

"Fire?" said Nikolus, then his eyes widened. "I remember now. The giant bird over the Pit of Fire! The ash from its wings…"

Falra! Tom thought.

The old man's eyes drifted closed again and he sagged back.

"Listen, I'm glad we could help you, but we have to be going now," Tom said. "As it happens, the Pit of Fire is our destination too."

As Tom securely fastened the bark shield to Storm's saddle and took his sword back from Elenna, Shay gripped his arm.

"Surely you can't be going where that bird monster lurks in the skies?" he asked.

Tom's throat and chest still felt raw from the smoke, but he ignored the pain as he fastened the buckle of his belt, tight.

"Yes," he said. "We're not afraid of a bird monster."

A MISTAKE

Nikolus shifted reluctantly again.
"Wait!" he said weakly.

We can't wait any longer, thought
Tom. *We've lost enough time...*

"Take these," said the old man. He
reached under his shirt and pulled
out a set of old beads on a string –
grey, misshapen pebbles.

"You don't need to offer us
payment," said Elenna.

Nikolus stood up quickly, his eyes suddenly alert. "You don't understand," he said. "You can't face the monster in the Pit of Fire without them. They'll protect you."

Tom managed a grateful smile. *No*

doubt he means well, but this is no time for old-fashioned superstitions and lucky charms.

The young boy Shay was staring at Nikolus, mouth agape. "Grandfather, what are you doing? You've had those beads for ever. You don't even take them off to sleep!"

Nikolus struggled to his feet. "There's much you don't understand, young lad," he replied. "If this warrior is who I think he is, he must take these."

The old man stared at Tom with a stern expression. Tom sensed a soldier's courage in the man's face, despite his wrinkles.

But does he really know I'm Master of the Beasts? he wondered.

Nikolus pressed the beads into Tom's hand. "Defeat this Beast for the good of Avantia," he said. Then he leaned in close and added quietly, "Son of Taladon."

A gasp caught in Tom's throat. "How do you...?"

The old man smiled, revealing a toothless mouth. "Let's just say you look a lot like your grandfather," he said. "Another hero in his time."

Elenna cut in. "Let's go now," she said. "The day is wearing on, and when darkness falls and the moon rises again, Vedra's struggle will be over."

Tom nodded grimly. "Thank you for these," he said to Nikolus. "You must let me give you something in return." He went to Storm, and unfastened the bark shield from the saddle, handing it to Shay. "The road back will be perilous," he said. "Hold this in front and the hot ash will not harm you."

The old man gave a slow nod. "Good luck."

Tom and Elenna mounted Storm and pressed on towards the heat haze of the Pit of Fire, pulling their tunics up over their mouth when the drifting ash was at its worst. They tied a scrap of cloth to Storm's bridle too, but could do nothing about the grey dust that coated his black flanks.

The air grew hotter, until beads of sweat began to trickle down Tom's spine. He scanned the sky, but there was no sign of Falra.

"Do you have a plan?" asked Elenna, clearly sensing his thoughts. "What if Falra won't come to us? All she has to do is stay hidden, and there will be nothing that we can do for Vedra. Kensa will have won."

Tom had been thinking ever since they left the boy and his grandfather. He had an idea, but he wasn't sure if it would work. "If Falra won't show herself, I'll lure her out with my shadow," he said. He tapped the white jewel in his belt, a token he'd won from Kaymon the Gorgon Hound countless Quests ago. It gave Tom the power to separate his shadow from his body.

"But while your shadow is off scouting for the Beast, you can't move," said Elenna. "You'll be vulnerable."

"It's a risk I have to take," Tom replied, grimly.

The edge of the Pit of Fire was still a hundred paces away when he reined Storm to a halt. The heat was so intense it was hard for Tom to keep his eyes open without blinking furiously. "Wait here with Storm," he said to Elenna. "Hopefully it won't be long until Falra decides to come out and fight."

Tom pressed the white jewel and concentrated. The sensation was always strange, as he watched his shadow peel away from his body. It slid off Storm's saddle and sprinted towards the Pit of Fire. Tom was left frozen on the stallion's back, controlling the shadow's progress with his mind. Though he could still feel his own body, he saw through the eyes of his shadow and heard with its ears. As it ran, he kept an eye out for the burnstone, the final magical ingredient that would complete the Gilded Elixir and free Vedra from Kensa's terrible enchantment.

Perhaps I can find the burnstone without even facing Falra, he thought. Deep down, though, he suspected Kensa was too cunning to make things that easy for him.

His shadow reached the edge of the Pit of Fire and stared down. The great hole in the ground seethed with fire and islands of black-red melting rock. Bubbles of lava hissed and popped, and sparks shot from the ground between twisting pathways of stone.

A place of death, Tom thought with a shiver down his back. *And just the place to find a phoenix.*

A huge mound rose from the centre of the molten rock. Something was pushing upwards from below.

SCREECH!

Tom's shadow saw a flash of white explode from the Pit of Fire. A shape rose up, feathers aflame and trailing ghostly ash.

Falra!

Smoke poured from the phoenix's

sharp beak, and lava spilled from her
sharp talons.

Tom's shadow staggered backwards.
Falra had grown so much since he'd
seen her in Rion. She was bigger
than Epos now, perhaps fifty arm-

lengths from wing tip to wing tip. Her talons alone could have torn down Uncle Henry's house.

Falra rose from the Pit of Fire, and for a moment her mighty form blocked out the sun. Then she wheeled around and flew straight over his shadow's head.

Panic shot through Tom's chest. The phoenix was flying straight towards Storm and Elenna. Her eyes were glassy orbs, blazing like flame – and they were sharply focused on Tom's immobile body.

The look they held was pure hatred.

She's going to kill me, Tom thought, *and there's nothing I can do to stop her!*

A FIERY PLUNGE

Quickly, Tom called his shadow back
to him using the jewel. The dark
outline began to run from the Pit of
Fire towards Storm. But Falra had
a head start. She flapped her flame-
tipped wings furiously, eating up
the sky.

My shadow's too slow, Tom thought.
It can't outrun the Beast.

"Elenna," Tom said urgently. "Push

me out of the saddle, and then go!"

"What?" she cried. "I can't leave you."

"Save yourself," said Tom, willing his shadow to run faster still. "Ride away on Storm."

"I've got a better idea!" Elenna said.

As Falra swooped down, Tom felt Elenna reach around his middle to grab the reins. She kicked Storm's flanks and wheeled around. The stallion set off at a gallop, with Falra in hot pursuit.

As the Beast descended, stretching out her talons, Elenna jerked the reins to one side and Storm veered left.

Falra swept past in a swoop of heat and ash, barely missing them.

"Take us towards my shadow!" Tom called back to Elenna. *If I can just*

reunite my body with its shadow,
perhaps we have a chance.

Storm's hooves pounded the ground as they charged towards the shadow.

But Falra turned as well, chasing the horse and riders. Tom's shadow saw the Beast sweep down behind them.

"Now!" he said to Elenna. "Throw me off before it's too late."

She shoved his body out of the saddle, and it landed with a thump on the ground. Tom felt a sting of pain as the lucky beads cut into his knuckles, but Falra's momentum carried her past his body.

His shadow ran faster still. *Just twenty paces between us.*

He readied himself to draw his sword. Soon Falra would be at his

mercy and he'd have the burnstone.

Ten paces.

Then Kensa will pay...

Tom's shadow leaped for his body, but at the same moment Falra swept down. The Beast's talons ripped into his clothes and snatched him into the sky.

"Noooo!" he cried.

The snow phoenix began to climb, turning back towards the Pit of Fire. As she beat her wings higher, Tom hung helplessly in her iron grip.

She's going to drop me into the lava, he thought. *She's carrying me to a fiery death!*

But then Tom saw that not all the Beast's feathers were the same gleaming white. One had turned black as coal, the sign of Kensa's poison. *If only I could use my sword,* he thought. *I'm close enough to reach it.*

Frustration tore at his mind. *But I can't move!* He saw his shadow standing below, by the side of a cliff-like ledge over the Pit of Fire. Unless it learned to fly, he couldn't see a way to reunite it with his body.

Falra soared over the Pit of Fire.
The rising heat made the hair on
Tom's arms start to singe and crinkle.

Then, through the baking winds,
Tom felt a sharp pain in his left hand.
He realised he was still holding the
old man's string of beads. But the
grey stones were glowing orange now,
heating up like embers.

Strange, thought Tom, hissing
through his teeth with pain. *It's as if
the Pit of Fire has awoken them.*

Another voice pushed into his
mind, and Tom realised it was
coming through the red jewel
in his belt. Falra was trying to
communicate with him.

It looks like you stumbled on the

burnstone, she said. *You've found the*
final ingredient. But you'll never get
to use it against me. Are you ready to
die now?

Falra turned lazily in the air. The
Pit of Fire bubbled and spat below.

"Tom!" Elenna called from the
saddle. "Can't you get free? Isn't there
anything you can do?"

The Beast started to fly in the
direction of his shadow. Summoning
all his energy, Tom sent a message to
his shadow. *Take a run up to the edge*
of the pit! As fast as you can!

Perhaps there was still a chance.

His shadow obeyed, sprinting
towards the top of the cliff.

"Just drop me!" Tom shouted to
Falra. "I'm fed up of your squawking."

Very well, she said. *Goodbye, so-called Master of the Beasts.*

Tom felt the talons release him and he plummeted downwards. At the same time, he saw through his shadow's eyes as it leaped off the lip of the fiery pit, reaching out its arms for his falling body.

They touched, and energy rushed back through Tom's limbs. *Yes!* They'd made it! He could move again. Legs flailing, he brought his shield over his head, focusing on the power of Arcta's eagle feather. At once he started to slow. The thermal currents caught the shield. He tilted it, and rode a current of air towards a shelf of rock at the edge of the pit. The heat was so intense he felt sure

his clothes would be set alight.

As his feet hit the rocky ground, he peered upwards through the smoke and saw Falra circling high above, shrieking to herself.

She thinks I'm dead, he thought.

Pain surged through Tom's hand.

He dropped the burnstone. The pebbles shone bright scarlet now.

They're close to home.

He remembered what Nikolus had said: *You can't face the monster in the Pit of Fire without them. They'll protect you.*

So there was some truth in his words! Falra had told him he'd never get the chance to use the charm against her, but she was wrong. They had to help in some way.

He glanced up at the mighty bird circling in the sky above him.

I have to get close to her, he thought. *If I'm going to defeat Falra, I need to face those talons again.*

THE BEGINNING OF THE END

Tom looped the beads over his belt, then laid his fingers on the red jewel and closed his eyes.

"Hear me, Falra!" he shouted.

The Beast answered from above with a screech, and then her voice sounded in Tom's head.

Impossible! I killed you!

"Think again," said Tom. "I'm down

here waiting for you, unless you're too scared to face me."

The snow phoenix directed her beak down and plunged through the smoke, eyes blazing.

I'm going to tear you limb from limb, she shrieked.

Tom readied himself, placing a hand on the hilt of his sword, though he had no plans to kill with it.

She has to think I'm serious, he thought, *or she'll realise it's a trap.*

Falra tipped her wings and hovered above him. The draughts from her enormous wings buffeted the air, almost knocking him off his feet.

"What are you waiting for?" he asked. "Kensa will be disappointed in you."

Falra screeched and extended her talons, scooping him off the rock. Tom found himself caught in her grasp for a second time.

Tom found himself fighting for breath, his arms pinned against his sides. *It wasn't supposed to be like this*. He needed to free his hand or the plan would fail!

They soared out of the flaming pit, but waves of heat from the Beast's feathers were making Tom feel woozy. He felt himself losing his grip on consciousness.

Must…fight…it, he told himself. He wriggled, and managed to shift one shoulder a little.

Kensa always said you were stupid, said Falra. *But even she didn't think you'd give yourself up this easily.*

Tom yanked his hand loose, and tugged the burnstone beads from his belt. The black feather was just above him. It looked charred and brittle.

If I can just reach it...

He saw Elenna on Storm's back. Her face was filled with horror as Falra swooped down towards them. His friend quickly laid an arrow against her bowstring.

That girl and her foolish darts, said Falra. *Does she really think—*

The words in Tom's head trailed off into a screech of agony as he swung the beads at her blackened feather. The feather sizzled and exploded into black dust. Falra's talons began to loosen their grip, and Tom felt himself falling.

Then, quite suddenly, the talons snatched closed again. With a powerful flick, Falra sent Tom spinning through the air. He landed on her back, legs astride her white feathers.

Don't worry, Tom, came her voice, clear and kind. *I've got you.*

Tom felt like punching the air as the phoenix soared over Elenna's head.

"It's all right!" he called down. "She's Good again!"

He saw the smile on Elenna's lips as she lowered her bow. Tom placed the burnstone beads in his satchel, along with the other magical ingredients.

Falra landed with a soft bump beside Storm and stretched out a wing. Tom ran along its length and leaped off. His stallion lowered his nose and nuzzled Tom's neck as Elenna clapped him on the back. "I saw you fall!" she said. "I thought... well, it looked as if..."

Tom grinned. "You should know by now that I'm quite hard to kill," he said. Elenna's own smile dropped as her gaze shifted over his shoulder. Tom spun around, just in time to see Falra's form fading to nothing.

"She's gone to protect another kingdom," Tom said. "And we should to get back to the palace with these ingredients." The sun was halfway to the horizon already.

"It's more than three days' ride from here," said Elenna. "We need Daltec's magic."

"Or maybe not," said Tom, pointing south. He saw a shape in the distance, shooting through the sky.

Elenna's face lit up. "Is that...?"

"Epos," Tom whispered.

His heart lifted at the magnificent sight. *The flame bird must have sensed we needed help!* The phoenix's beak and talons shone like gold in the sun's rays, and fire rippled over her tawny wings. In no time at all, her huge shadow engulfed them. Epos folded her wings and landed on the ground. She nodded her beak in greeting.

"Thank you for coming!" said Tom. "We need you to fly like the wind!"

Epos extended a wing and Elenna climbed on first. Tom led Storm up as well, and the stallion quickly settled between the flame bird's wings.

Tom felt a thrill as the phoenix took flight, pushing off from the ground with a powerful thrust of her legs.

Epos flew faster than Tom had ever known. He leaned close to her feathers as they cut through the blasting gusts of wind. Soon they were soaring over the Grassy Plains of central Avantia. Tom kept glancing sideways at the sun, now an orange orb almost touching the horizon. In the east, the sky had begun to fade to deep blue.

The moon will rise soon, Tom thought. *Perhaps the first one Vedra will see through Evil eyes.*

But they were making good progress. With no hindrance, they would make it to the palace in time to give Vedra the Gilded Elixir.

As the City finally came into view, Tom began to feel hope building in

his chest. *We've done it. The Quest is over...*

Just then a streak of flame rose from below. Epos veered sideways, and the spurt narrowly missed them. Tom almost rolled off the

Beast's back, but seized a handful of feathers to steady himself.

"What's going on?" yelled Elenna.

Tom's blood ran cold as he saw the shape emerge from a clearing. A dragon. Though the scales were black as night, he recognised the shape of the wings at once.

Krimon. Once he'd had a glorious red coat, but now Evil had turned his scales black.

On the dragon's back sat a familiar figure. She clutched a whip with a silver handle, and her long grey cloak flapped in the wind.

"Going somewhere, Tom?" cried Kensa gleefully.

CRASH LANDING

Epos keened in panic and flew on, but Kensa lashed Krimon's scales cruelly.

"Faster!" she cried.

The black dragon roared in pain but put on a burst of speed, flying alongside Epos.

"Did you really think you'd won?" Kensa shouted. "Did you think I'd let you simply fly home?"

Elenna crouched against Epos's

wing, an arrow to her bow. She loosed
the shaft, but Krimon roared a jet
of flame that caught it in mid-flight.
Tom gasped as the arrow turned to
falling ash.

"Don't waste your arrows, girl," said the sorceress scornfully.

Tom looked up at the tall walls of King Hugo's city growing ever closer. *I just have to keep Kensa distracted,* he thought.

"We have all the ingredients for the Gilded Elixir," he shouted. "Soon Vedra will be Good again, and we'll drive you from this kingdom for ever."

"You may have the elixir," said Kensa, cackling, "but you'll never give it to Vedra. When the moon rises, he'll be mine as well. With two dragons, I'll be unstoppable!"

"While there's blood in my veins, I'll always stop you," yelled Tom.

Kensa smiled. "Let's make that blood boil, shall we?"

She raised her whip and brought it down with a terrible crack across Krimon's neck. The Beast released a stream of fire towards them. Epos lurched, lifting a wing to protect Tom and Elenna. The flames flowed over her feathers harmlessly.

At the same time, Tom heard a cry and saw Elenna tumbling across Epos's back. His heart sank as she rolled off, but at the last moment her hand closed over feathers and kept her from falling. Screaming, she dangled over nothing, holding onto life with a single hand. Tom started to move over towards her, crawling across Epos's huge back.

"Just what I like!" said Kensa. "An easy target!" She guided Krimon to

Epos's other side. "She can't help you now!" said Kensa triumphantly. "But she can watch Krimon cook you."

Krimon opened his mouth, and Tom saw flames building in the dragon's throat.

What can I do?

Then it hit him.

"Elenna, catch!" he said, taking off his shield and sending it spinning towards her.

She snatched the shield with one hand just as Krimon blasted fire towards her. Elenna's face twisted in a grimace as the flames poured over the shield and bounced back, reflected by Ferno's scale.

"Fly, Epos!" yelled Tom. "As fast as you can!"

The flame bird somehow found
a burst of speed and carried them
away from Krimon and his Evil
rider. Tom clambered back to where
Elenna was hanging and reached
down. He managed to heave her back
up onto Epos's back. Tom saw that
her left sleeve was slightly burned,
the skin raw beneath.

"Are you all right?" he said,
nodding at the wound.

"It could have been a lot worse,"
she said, managing a flicker of a
smile as she handed back his shield.

Krimon was still following, too far
back to reach them with his fire. In
the west, the sun was just an arc over
the horizon. The air had grown cold.

"We can't let Krimon get into the

City," said Elenna. "Hundreds will die."

"And we can't face him out here in the open," said Tom. "He's too agile under Kensa's control."

He chewed his lips, trying to think of a plan. The City lay not far ahead, the walls rising pale over the moat.

"I've got an idea," he said. "Hold on tight. Look after Storm."

He glanced back. Krimon was gaining again, Kensa cruelly lashing him over and over.

Tom grasped the red jewel. "Epos!" he said. "Fly low, at the walls."

The Beast responded at once, drifting down so she shot just above the open plains.

"Tom, what are you doing?" asked Elenna, as they closed on the City.

Doubts from Epos's mind also flooded Tom's.

"Trust me," Tom told them both. "Epos, go faster!"

Epos's wings beat harder still. The fields below moved past in a blur. Tom risked a look behind.

Krimon was almost in range, smoke streaming from his nostrils. Kensa's eyes drilled into him with pure hatred.

"Tom, we're not high enough," called Elenna worriedly.

All Tom could see were the City's walls ahead.

Forty paces.

"Tom, we're going to crash!" said Elenna.

"No, we're not..." Tom muttered.

Thirty paces.

He heard Kensa cry out, "Scorch them, Krimon!"

At twenty paces, Tom suddenly yanked on Epos's neck feathers and yelled, "Pull up!"

With a desperate screech, the flame bird heaved back her wings and stretched her neck skyward. She tucked up her talons and soared over the battlements.

Kensa had no time to react. Tom glanced down and saw Krimon slam into the walls with a thunderous impact. Stone crumpled and a whole section of the defences toppled down over the Beast. In the billowing clouds of dust, he couldn't see Kensa.

Alarm bells began to ring across

the City as Epos landed in the
central courtyard. Lanterns lit up
behind shutters and panicked shouts
rose from all around.

"What was that?"

"It sounded like an explosion!"

Tom leaped off Epos's back and led Storm down quickly.

"Do you think they're...dead?" asked Elenna.

Tom's breath was coming hard. *If I've killed a Good Beast, I don't know if I can live with myself.* But there were other, urgent matters to consider, too. Vedra. They had to use the four ingredients to liberate him from Evil – now!

He laid a hand on Epos's beak. "Fly away!" he told the flame bird. "The people must not see you."

Epos turned a fierce eye on Tom. *She doesn't want to leave.*

"You must go," said Tom, stroking his friend's feathers. "Thank you. Without you, Avantia would be doomed."

As the first soldier ran out of the barracks, his armour rattling, Epos lifted off and flew away, becoming a distant dot in the sky.

"Come on!" Tom said, turning to Elenna. "We have to deliver the ingredients before it's too late."

8

EVIL BLOOD

Clutching the satchel in his fist, Tom sprinted across the courtyard towards a narrow set of stairs that led downwards. Only one part of the palace had been big enough to conceal Vedra safely – the vast, stone cellars underground.

Elenna ran at his side, trying to avoid the soldiers swarming out of their barracks. Captain Harkman was yelling orders, his face flushed.

"Form ranks!" he shouted. "Weapons ready! Stay calm!"

He saw Tom charging past and he gave a nod of acknowledgment. The captain was one of the few people trusted by the king to know the truth about the Beasts. "Make way for Tom and Elenna!" he cried.

As Tom reached the stairs, Daltec emerged from the palace doors.

"Tom, Elenna! You made it!" said the young wizard. "Do you have all the ingredients?"

"Here," said Tom. As he handed the satchel to Daltec, his eyes landed on a figure in the doorway. King Hugo was strapping on his polished silver breastplate. He was dressed from

head to toe in armour. He wore his
sword belt as well.

"Kensa and Krimon crashed into
the walls," Tom said. "I don't know if
they're alive."

"You take care of Vedra," said the
king, grimly, drawing his sword. "I'll

defend my castle and see to those two!"

"Take Storm," said Tom. "He's the best stallion in Avantia."

The king nodded.

"Follow me," said Daltec, heading down the stairs.

Tom and Elenna followed, and gasped when they reached the bottom. The chamber was dark but for a few candles lit around the walls. Even in the gloom, Tom could tell that Vedra had changed almost beyond recognition. His scales, once emerald green, were now completely black, as if his entire body had been scorched by fire.

"We're too late," Tom whispered, turning to Elenna.

"Perhaps not," said a voice. Tom

spun round and saw Aduro sitting on a chair at the side of the room. His face was lined with deep grooves of worry, and the dark shadows beneath his eyes made Tom think the old man hadn't slept for a long time.

He's been keeping watch down here since we left on our Quest.

Daltec had already set up a wide silver dish over an iron tripod. Now he added the ingredients – the starleaf from the Murmuring Peak, and a few leaves of the hidden tree from the Dark Jungle. Over the top he poured the flask of water from the City of Snakes in the far reaches of the Ruby Desert. Last of all he placed the burnstones beneath the dish.

His lips moved in a silent

incantation, and the stones burst
into flame. It seemed to take for ever,
but eventually the water began to
boil, melting the plants in the dish to
a brown sludge.

Tom glanced at Elenna. His friend
looked unsure, and he felt the same

way. *Can this really work?*

But then the mixture seemed to change colour, turning a rich gold, like liquid sunlight.

Daltec looked up from the dish with a grim expression. "I need you both to open the dragon's mouth."

Tom swallowed, and stepped forward with his friend. Vedra's jaws were huge, large enough to snatch him up in a single bite. The dragon's eyes were just glistening slits. Shallow breath drifted from his nostrils.

Maybe he's turned already, Tom thought. *If we wake him, he might devour us all.*

Elenna hesitated a few paces from the dragon, clearly thinking the same.

We have to try, thought Tom.

He nodded to his friend.

Elenna took the lower jaw, and Tom gripped the cold scales of the upper one. Gritting his teeth, he pushed upwards. They managed to prise the jaws open with a creak like a rusted hinge, to reveal teeth as long as Tom's arm. Vedra didn't even stir.

"Quickly!" said Tom, straining. "I can't hold this for long, even with the power of my golden breastplate."

Daltec gripped the handles of the dish and carried it over. He wasted no time in pouring the mixture into the Beast's mouth. The Gilded Elixir sizzled as it rolled down the groove in Vedra's blackened tongue.

Nothing happened.

Tom couldn't hold the dragon's

jaw open any more and lowered it,
stepping back with Elenna.

Daltec set down the dish and ran
his fingers through his hair. Aduro
shuffled slowly forward. "We did our

best," he said, placing a hand on his apprentice's shoulder. "Sometimes Evil prevails…"

A low rumble from Vedra's throat shook the air and the dragon's eyes flicked open. Glassy black orbs stared at Tom. His heart sank in despair. Then the Beast's head jerked upwards and his huge tail whipped from under his body, scattering the dish and the remains of the elixir. Tom's hand went to the hilt of his sword by instinct.

"Tom, no!" said Elenna quickly, grabbing his arm. "Look!"

She was pointing at Vedra's eye. Tom saw it too. In the depths of the oily stare, there was a flicker of green.

Vedra flexed his jaws, and in his

throat red fire sparked. *If he breathes his fire in this cellar, we'll all be burned to death,* thought Tom. His hand tightened on his sword hilt, but he didn't draw it. Vedra's eyes narrowed, black again.

He's fighting the poison...

Tom laid his other hand on his red jewel. "Come back to us, old friend," he whispered. "Let your goodness win through."

Vedra's head thrashed from side to side, as if he was shaking loose bad thoughts which lurked there.

Daltec and Aduro stepped back.

"I don't think it's working," said the young wizard, his voice quavering uncertainly.

Vedra rose up on his haunches, and

the fire from his throat grew hotter.

"Tom, maybe we should run," said Elenna.

But Tom released his sword completely, and closed his eyes, focusing all his mind on the red jewel. He felt the heat of the dragon's breath on his face.

"I saved you when you were still in your egg," he said. "You must trust me now. You're Good, Vedra. A Good Beast of Rion."

Tom heard the others gasp. He opened his eyes to see Vedra's head right in front of his own. His heart thumped in awe.

The dragon's shining scales were green again!

BROTHERS AT WAR

"We did it!" Elenna cried.

Vedra turned his kindly stare on the others, his eyes bright.

Aduro glanced upwards, and Tom heard it too. Shouts of panic were drifting down from ground level.

"Kensa!" said Tom. "We have to get up there and fight!"

"Your wish is my command," said Daltec. With a wave of his hand, the cellar vanished. Tom found his hands tightening on…green scales!

Tom found himself soaring high above the palace, sitting astride Vedra's back. A full moon glowed in the sky, casting everything in a light, silvery glow.

But the sight below him chilled Tom's blood.

On the ground, Kensa was guiding Krimon towards the soldiers on the wall. The dragon looked unharmed, as did the sorceress riding him. Many parts of the palace were already on fire from the attack. King Hugo galloped across the courtyard on Storm's back, bellowing commands at his men.

As Tom watched, Krimon directed a jet of flame at those defending the

outer wall, and they ducked beneath
the battlements to avoid being
torched. One wasn't so lucky. With
his arm aflame, he leaped into the
moat below, coming up gasping
for breath.

The remaining soldiers stood and launched a volley of arrows, but Krimon was already wheeling away and the shafts fell short.

"We have to stop them!" Tom cried. Vedra knew what to do and swooped downwards, talons extended.

Kensa saw them coming and steered Krimon to face them.

"Roast them, my pet!" she screeched.

Cruelty filled Krimon's black eyes as he opened his mouth and blasted fire. Vedra turned and batted the flames back with his wing.

Tom saw his chance as the dragons almost collided. He pushed off with his legs and landed with a thump behind Kensa on Krimon's bony back. He wrapped an arm around the

sorceress's shoulders, trying to drag
her off.

"It's over, Kensa!" he hissed to her.

"Never!" she cried.

Tom just saw her elbow come up
before pain exploded in his nose.
Stars filled his vision and he lost
his grip.

I'm going to fall!

He drew his sword, jamming it into
Krimon's scales to stop himself.

The Beast roared with rage.
Through watery, blurred vision,
Tom saw Krimon's long neck arch
round. He blinked away his tears to
see terrifying jaws snarling an arm's
length from his face.

Dodging them, Tom began to
clamber towards Kensa. Wind

whistled past as he clawed hand over hand up the dragon's back.

Suddenly, Krimon jerked sideways, throwing Tom off his feet. The air rushed from Tom's lungs as he landed. He rolled over the Beast's wing joint, reaching desperately with his hands. His fingertips found the edge of a scale and he dangled helplessly off the Beast's flank. He looked up and saw Kensa looming over him. She planted her feet apart, balancing perfectly on the flying dragon. She raised one leather boot and placed her heel on Tom's fingers.

A smile spread over her bloodless lips. "I'm going to enjoy this," she said, peering down at him. "Happy landing, Tom."

She pressed her weight on Tom's fingers. He winced in agony as she ground at his bones.

"So brave," said Kensa. "You never did know when to give up." She reached for the whip at her waist. "A couple of lashes with this might dent your courage."

Kensa raised the deadly whip, her face twisted in the moonlight.

Then she screamed as white fire streamed in front of Tom's eyes.

When he dared to look again, Kensa had gone.

Vedra shot past, smoke still trailing from his jaws. *He killed her!* Tom thought, aghast. He dragged himself up onto Krimon's back.

Through the red jewel, he heard

the green dragon's voice, directed
forcefully at Krimon.

*My brother, stop this destruction!
We are the protectors of Avantia, not
her enemies!*

Krimon turned to his twin and
snapped his jaws.

I will save you, brother, said Vedra,
*but it will hurt. I must burn away
your Evil.*

Never! replied Krimon. *Kensa is
my mistress until I die!*

He breathed a spurt of fire at Vedra,
but the green dragon rose above it,
climbing high into the sky.

Where's he going? Tom wondered.

For a moment Vedra was a
silhouette against the moon, then he
dipped his head and dived.

Shield yourself, Master of the Beasts! said his voice.

Tom understood what the green dragon was about to do. He crouched against Krimon's back and raised his shield. *Ferno's scale is about to be tested like never before,* he thought.

Krimon's head turned up and he saw his brother shooting through the sky. Tom gritted his teeth.

When the two dragons were a wing's length apart, Vedra opened his mouth wide.

Tom raised his shield arm as a torrent of white fire engulfed him.

10

A FRIEND RETURNS

The air around Tom seemed to burn
and he heard Krimon's shrieks of
pain as the flames swamped him.

Then, just as quickly, the heat was
gone, and cool air flowed around
them once more.

Tom blinked and didn't understand
for a moment what he was seeing.

Red scales...

Realisation dawned as Krimon's

voice pushed its way into his mind.

My brother saved me, Master of the Beasts. With his white fire, he made me Good again.

Tom's heart swelled with joy as his eyes took in Krimon's gleaming red scales. Vedra flew alongside, roaring with triumph. Together, the twin dragons started to glide down towards the palace courtyard.

Hundreds of archers turned their bows on the sky. Tom's chest tightened with fear.

"Don't fire!" he cried. "Krimon is with us again!"

King Hugo bellowed, "Hold your fire!" from Storm's back, and the soldiers lowered their bows.

Krimon and Vedra landed in the

midst of the archers, who cowered
back. The king reined Storm to a
halt and the stallion snorted long
steaming breaths.

It's not every day they see a Beast,
thought Tom, *let alone two!*

At that moment, four more soldiers
rode into the courtyard. With them

came Elenna, riding Breeze.

King Hugo dismounted as Aduro and Daltec arrived at his side.

What's going on? Tom wondered.

"Report," said the king.

Elenna slid down from the saddle and bowed her head before the king.

"Your Majesty, we found no trace of the sorceress."

Tom frowned. "Kensa?"

King Hugo nodded. "I sent out a search party. We saw her fall from the dragon's back. I wanted to capture her."

"The fire," said Tom, recalling the fierce white flame. "It was hot enough to melt metal, I'm sure. Perhaps she's...dead."

Aduro stepped past them, looking out into the sky. "Perhaps," he said quietly. "I would have liked to see her brought to justice for her crimes."

"She faced justice of a sort," said King Hugo. "Our kingdom is rid of her, at least."

Aduro smiled thinly.

The soldiers let out a collective gasp as Vedra shot a jet of flame into the sky. Krimon did the same, matching his twin.

King Hugo laughed. "To think, we kept the secret of the Beasts for so long. There's no denying it now, though, is there?"

Tom grinned too, but then a realisation hit him.

"Why haven't they disappeared?" he asked. The other Beasts of Rion had vanished when they had been freed from Kensa's wicked curse.

"Well," began Aduro, "it's because... Oh," he said, catching himself. "Really I should let young Daltec explain. He's your guide now."

Blood rushed to Daltec's cheeks. "The Beasts of Rion each have new kingdoms to guard, but the twin dragons are Beasts of Avantia now," he said. "They will serve alongside Epos and the others."

"Hey...come back here!" shouted a voice.

Tom and the others spun around. By the palace gates, a number of soldiers were scampering back and forth in confusion.

"Stop that creature!" said another. *Another Beast?* Tom drew his

sword, but then a grey shape leaped
over a soldier's outstretched arm.

"Silver!" cried Elenna.

The wolf howled and ran to her.

Elenna dropped to her knees and
wrapped her arms tightly around
his neck. "You made it home!" she

said. "I never doubted you!"

Tom slid his sword into his scabbard, smiling. King Hugo laid a hand on his shoulder.

"It seems my kingdom is at peace again, thanks to you both."

Tom didn't know what to say.

"But you have also let me down," continued the king, his face suddenly turning grave.

Tom swallowed and fell to his knees. "How so?" he asked.

"You disobeyed my strict command," said the king.

Tom frowned. "Your Majesty, everything I've done has been for the good of Avantia. If I've disappointed you in some way, please tell me."

He looked up to see the king

fighting a smile. "I ordered you to go home and rest, remember?" he said.

Aduro chuckled, and Tom's heart lifted. "I remember, Your Majesty," he said, "but some small tasks got in the way." He glanced at the two dragons.

"Well, the order still stands," said the king, smiling. "Are you ready to undertake your next Quest – to put your feet up at last?"

Tom stood again, and undid his sword belt. "While there's blood in my veins," he said with a grin, "I will do my best."

THE END

CONGRATULATIONS, YOU HAVE COMPLETED THIS QUEST!

At the end of each chapter you were awarded a special gold coin. The QUEST in this book was worth an amazing 11 coins.

Look at the Beast Quest totem picture inside the back cover of this book to see how far you've come in your journey to become

MASTER OF THE BEASTS.

The more books you read, the more coins you will collect!

Do you want your own
Beast Quest Totem?
1. Cut out and collect the coin below
2. Go to the Beast Quest website
3. Download and print out your totem
4. Add your coin to the totem
www.beastquest.co.uk/totem

11

Don't miss the
first exciting
Beast Quest book
in this series,
RAFFKOR THE
STAMPEDING
BRUTE!
Read on for a
sneak peek...

CHAPTER ONE

TOM'S REWARD

Storm lowered his head over the door of the stall as Tom fed him an apple.

"Eat up, boy," he said. "You deserve more than just a treat and new shoes, but that will have to do for now."

"It's good to be together again, isn't it?" said Elenna. She was sitting on a hay bale, tightening her bowstring. Silver lounged beside her.

Tom nodded. He'd walked the Warrior's Road without his beloved steed, and had occasionally doubted they would ever be reunited. He'd only just triumphed on his last Quest.

A palace steward knocked at the stable door. "If you please, young sir and lady," he said, "His Majesty requests your presence in the banqueting hall."

"Of course!" said Elenna, leaping up. "I'd almost forgotten about dinner with King Hugo."

Tom ruffled Storm's mane and they followed the steward to the palace.

When the steward threw open
the tall wooden doors, Tom gasped.
He'd expected just King Hugo, the
wizard, Daltec, and Aduro, but
the hall was packed with people.
Courtiers, servants and soldiers filled
the benches. Candles blazed in their
holders and the tables groaned under
the weight of platters of roasted
meats, wheels of cheese and piles
of fruit.

King Hugo stood up, raising
a goblet. The room burst into
wild applause. Flushing with
embarrassment, Tom whispered, "Is
this all for us?"

Elenna's eyes were wide. "It looks
like it," she said.

"Let the festivities begin!" cried

King Hugo, gesturing to the empty seats either side of him.

Tom and Elenna made their way through the crowd as people patted them on the back. Even Captain Harkman managed a smile, though it looked a little like a grimace. "Good to have you home, Tom," he said.

Tom settled into the seat beside the king, and lowered his voice. "Surely this isn't all for me and Elenna," he asked, looking around.

King Hugo grinned. "It's a double celebration," he said. "Your successful Quest, as well as the anniversary of my coronation."

Aduro smiled and rose from his seat, lifting his goblet. "A toast!" the former wizard declared. "To King Hugo's

many years on the throne, and to
many more!"

Tom and Elenna raised their cups
of fruit juice and joined in with the
room's chorus.

"To King Hugo!"

Time seemed to fly past. Tom ate until his stomach felt close to bursting. Elenna passed scraps of meat beneath the table to Silver.

As the platters were cleared away, the music grew louder, drowning out the voices of the feasters. Tumblers and acrobats began to perform in front of the guests.

King Hugo had retired to bed and Tom's eyelids were starting to droop as he watched a fire-breather. *I can't remember the last time I felt this tired,* he thought. Then he noticed Daltec beckoning to him from the far side of the room.

What can he want?

Tom nudged Elenna. "I think something's wrong."

Silver yawned and got up, leaving the bone he'd been gnawing. Tom led the way towards the young wizard.

"Is it Jezrin the Judge?" Tom asked. Their enemy had vanished when they returned from the Warrior's Road, his evil plans defeated. "Has there been any news of him?"

"We've heard nothing," said Daltec, shaking his head. "The Circle of Wizards has banished him from their number. Aduro believes it will be some time before he regains enough strength to attack the kingdom again."

"Then what's wrong?" Elenna asked, worriedly.

Daltec nodded. "Follow me."

He led them through a side door and along a narrow, unlit corridor. The air was cool after the crowded banqueting hall, and the sounds of the celebration grew muted.

They reached the end of the passage, and Daltec drew aside a heavy curtain. On the other side was a small chamber lit by a fire burning in the hearth. King Hugo sat in a chair in the centre of the room. *So he's not in bed after all!* Aduro stood leaning on a staff at his side.

The king stood up. "I have a mission for you both," he said.

Read
RAFFKOR THE STAMPEDING
BRUTE
to find out more!

FIGHT THE BEASTS,
FEAR THE MAGIC

Are you a BEAST QUEST mega fan?
Do you want to know about all the latest news,
competitions and books before anyone else?

Then join our Quest Club!

Visit the BEAST QUEST website
and sign up today!

www.beastquest.co.uk

Are you a collector of the
Beast Quest cards?

Go to www.beastquest.co.uk
for more details.

Discover the new Beast Quest mobile game fro...

Available free on iOS and Android

Guide Tom on his Quest to free the Good Beasts
of Avantia from Malvel's evil spells.

Battle the Beasts, defeat the minions,
unearth the secrets and collect
rewards as you journey through the
Kingdom of Avantia.

DOWNLOAD THE APP TO BEGIN
THE ADVENTURE NOW!

JAN   2017